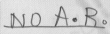

OL

NO A·R·

This book belongs to

The Adventures of
Bella & Harry
Let's Visit London!

Written By
Lisa Manzione

Illustrated By
Kristine Lucco

Bella & Harry, LLC

www.BellaAndHarry.com
email: BellaAndHarryGo@aol.com

Hurry, hurry!! The jousting event is just beginning! I can't wait to see Knight Harry!

Just as the crowd arrived, Knight Harry rode in on his beautiful white horse.

Hooray! Hooray!
    The crowd cheered...

"Harry! Harry! Wake up!
We are in London, England and our tour
is ready to start."

"Bella?"

"I was dreaming I was a famous knight! I was just starting a jousting match!"

"A jousting match?
Harry, you don't know anything
about jousting."

"Hummm.....Bella,
what exactly is jousting?"

"Jousting is a very old form of competition. Knights rode horses, usually carrying long poles, and tried to push the other person off his horse. I don't think we will see any jousting events today."

9

"Today, jousting events are just for fun. Hundreds of years ago the events were held to determine who was the strongest knight or warrior."

"I am a very strong puppy! I would have won ALL of the matches!"

"Yes, Harry, I am sure you would have won all of the jousting matches, but we need to board the tour bus with our family. We are off to see the sights and sounds of London."

TOUR BUS

"Bella,

where exactly is London?"

"London is located in the country of England, which is located in Great Britain. Great Britain also includes Scotland and Wales."

SCOTLAND

NORTH SEA

ATLANTIC OCEAN

IRELAND

ENGLAND

WALES

12

"**Let's** look at the map together so we know exactly where we are before we start our tour."

LONDON

"This is a fun way to begin the tour! Our family is riding on a red double decker bus!"

"First stop... Big Ben!"

"Bella, who is Ben?"

"Ben is not a person. Big Ben is a four sided clock that has kept almost exact time since the clock was set in motion in 1859."

16

"Big Ben
is the largest clock
in Great Britain.
Including the tower,
Big Ben is approximately
320 feet tall or about
53 cows standing
tail to tail!"

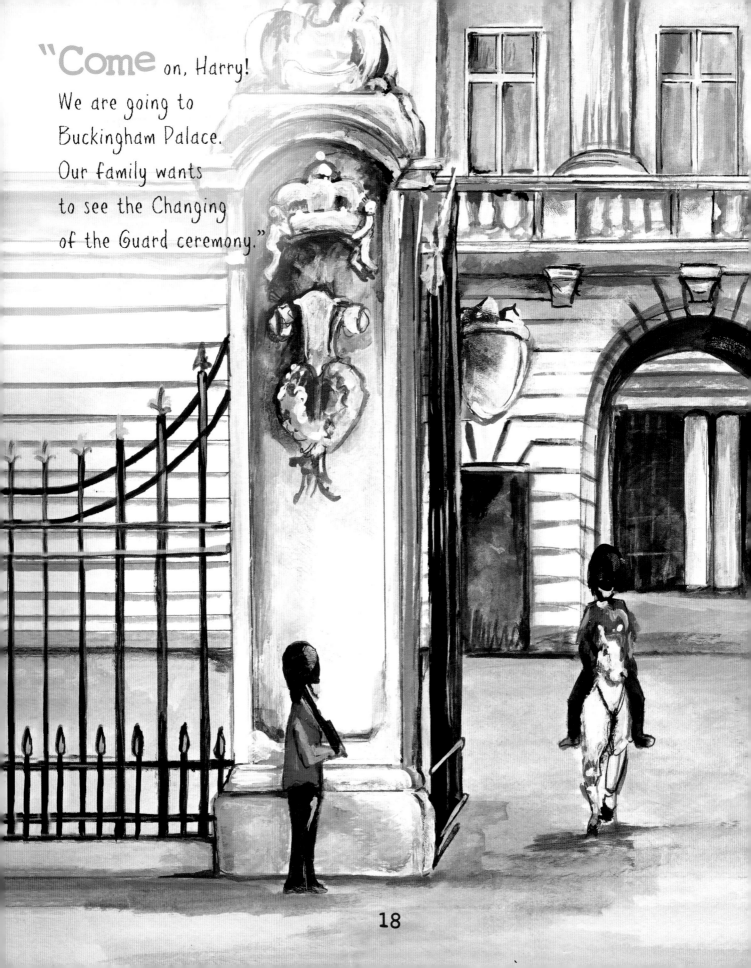

"Come on, Harry!
We are going to
Buckingham Palace.
Our family wants
to see the Changing
of the Guard ceremony."

18

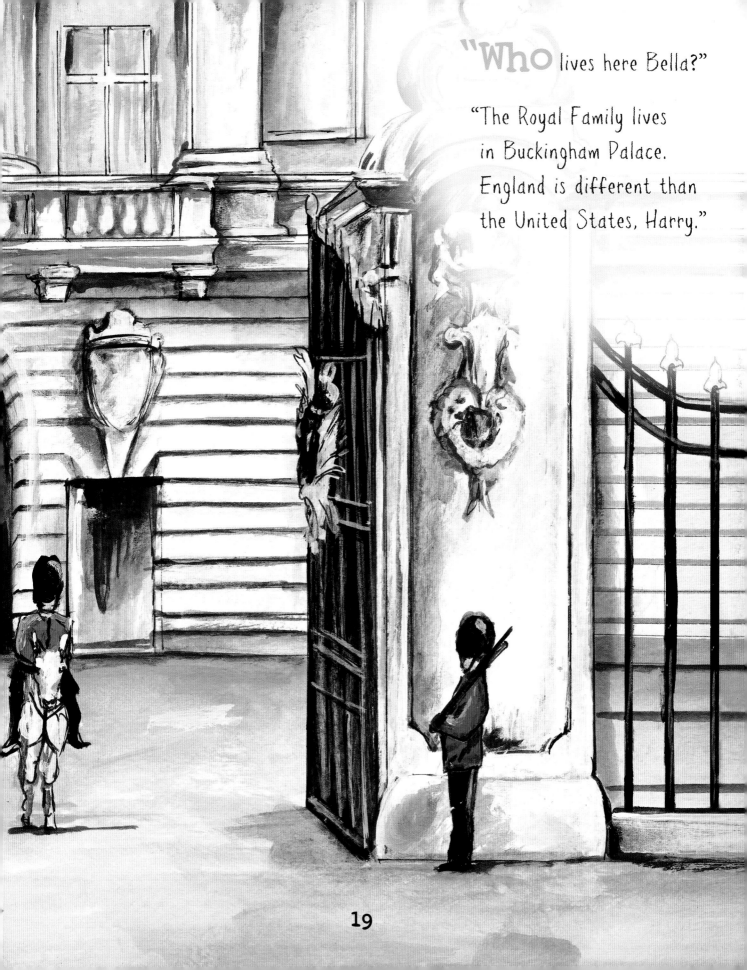

"Who lives here Bella?"

"The Royal Family lives
in Buckingham Palace.
England is different than
the United States, Harry."

"In America we have a President who runs the country along with several other branches of government. England has a King and a Queen who help run the country, along with several other leaders that represent the people who live in Great Britain and its territories."

"Harry, look! It's the Changing of the Guard ceremony!"

"Look at me, Bella! I am going to march with the guards!"

"Harry, come back here! The guards cannot play with you while they are on duty. The guards have a very important job and that job is taken very seriously. They are responsible for guarding the official residence of the Royal Family."

"Bella, look at the cool hats the guards are wearing!"

"Harry, the hats are made of real bearskin and weigh about one and a half pounds. That is too heavy for a puppy to wear!"

"Bella, look over there!
I see London Bridge!"

"Yes, Harry, you see a bridge,
but it is not the London Bridge
we sing about in the song.
It is the Tower Bridge.
It is called the Tower Bridge
because it is very close
to the Tower of London."

"The original London Bridge was moved to Lake Havasu, Arizona, USA, several years ago. The old London Bridge was sinking into the Thames River and it had to be replaced."

"Ohhhhhh..."

25

"**Harry,** the bus is stopping at the London Waterloo Train Station. We will be boarding the train and riding it to the Salisbury Train Station. When we leave the Salisbury Train Station we will be going to see one of the most famous sites in history!"

26

"But first, we must settle down in our train seats. It's snack time. The children are having tea and crumpets!"

"Crumpets? What are crumpets?"

"Well Harry, crumpets are similar to cookies or biscuits."

"**Bella,** I see rocks standing up straight from the ground."

"Harry, those are not just any rocks, those rocks
are the famous site called Stonehenge."

28

"It is still a mystery as to why Stonehenge was built, but it is a very important part of history."

"The children want to play hide and seek with us. You are it, Bella! Find us if you can!"

"**Whew!** Harry, that was so much fun, but it looks like we are leaving now. We need to go back to the train station and board the train for dinner and a relaxing ride back to London."

"What's for dinner, Bella?"

"It looks like fish and chips tonight. Fish and chips is a very common meal served in England. The fish is usually fried and the chips are what we call french fries in the United States."

"That sounds great! You know I LOVE french fries!"

31

Our bags are packed and it is time to leave London.
We are off to another exciting city for fun and adventure with our family.
Won't you come along? We hope so! But for now... "cheerio",
or "good bye", from Bella Boo and Harry too!

Our Adventure to London

Bella and Harry standing
by the red phone booth.

Bella & Harry playing in Hyde Park
where they met a Cavalier King Charles
Spaniel, Jackson.

Bella and Harry riding
in the London Eye.

Bella with one of the Queen's guards.

Bella & Harry in their hotel room
looking out on Piccadilly Circus.

Bella & Harry crossing Abbey Road.

Bella & Harry looking up
at Westminster Abbey.

Bella & Harry at the Tower of London.

34

Common British Words and Phrases

Lift – Elevator   Queue – Line

Bobby – Policeman   Chap – Man

Boot – Car trunk   Cheerio! – Good bye!

Loo – Restroom

I love fairy cakes! – I love cupcakes!

Where is the lift? – Where is the elevator?

You are the bee's knees! – You are fantastic!

Library of Congress Cataloging-in-Publications Data is available

Manzione, Lisa

The Adventures of Bella & Harry: Let's Visit London!

ISBN: 978-1-937616-03-8

First Edition

Book Three of Bella & Harry Series

For further information please visit:

www.BellaAndHarry.com

or

Email: BellaAndHarryGo@aol.com

CPSIA Section 103 (a) Compliant

www.beaconstar.com/ consumer

ID: L0118329. Tracking No.: L1312347-7926

Printed in China